SHULAMITH

SHULAMITH

JULIA STEIN

West End Press

Acknowledgments are made to the following publications where these poems have appeared: *Beyond Lament: Poets of the World Bearing Witness to the Holocaust* (Northwestern University Press); *Earth's Daughters*; *Jewish Women's Literary Annual; minnesota review; Mosaic: A Jewish Literary Magazine; Pearl*; and *Verve*.

First edition May 2002
ISBN 0-9705344-3-4

Book and cover design by Nancy Woodard
Author photo by David Brown

Distributed by University of New Mexico Press

West End Press • P.O. Box 27334 • Albuquerque, New Mexico 87125

CONTENTS

INTRODUCTION

Shulamith as a book of poems was inspired in the 1970s when I attended a number of conferences about Jewish women at UCLA Hillel. Before attending these conferences, as a young poet I felt I was an orphan born from a male line of writers. I thought only men created midrash, exposition of the Bible, and the only Jewish writers in English, Hebrew or Yiddish were men. I was raised next door to my Russian Jewish grandmother, but she told me only bits and pieces about her life and never taught me her language, Yiddish. I felt like the granddaughter in Tillie Olsen's story "Tell Me A Riddle," who had never learned her own heritage.

All this changed at the UCLA Hillel conferences. I was lucky enough to hear such pioneering women as Rabbi Laura Geller, then a rabbinic student, and Rachel Adler, a theologian, speak about spirituality, as well as historian Norma Fein Pratt talk about her researches recovering Yiddishe women writers. I eagerly collected the early publications of this Jewish women's movement: *Response* magazine's 1973 "The Jewish Woman: An Anthology," *Lilith* magazine, and Norma Fein Pratt's handouts of poems by Yiddishe women newly translated into English. It was inspiring to hear Adler, a woman, create commentary on the Bible from a woman's point of view. It was inspiring to learn for the first time from Pratt that I had poetic mothers in Yiddish: Kadia Molodowsky, Celia Dropkin, Anna Margolin and others. I was surprised to read Adrienne Rich's translations of Molodowsky's and Dropkin's poems.

In the late 1970s at one UCLA Hillel Conference I joined with a few other Jewish women to form a study group. For a year we studied Jewish women's history and literature. Another discovery I made was a volume of *TriQuarterly* magazine called "Contemporary Israeli Literature." In this anthology I read for the first time a number of Israeli women poets: Raquel Chalfi; Esther Raab; Dahlia Ravikovitch; and Zelda (I had earlier discovered Hebrew poet Leah Goldberg).

The researches I had done in the 1970s and early 1980s were reflected in the poems in my first book *Under the Ladder to Heaven,* published in 1984. In this book I had two poems in the voices of Biblical women: a Lilith poem and a poem about an anonymous woman who wrestles with an angel just as Jacob had. *Under the Ladder to Heaven* included numerous poems about the Yiddish American women who had organized the garment workers' union 1909-1915. I also had more personal poems about my great-grandmother, my grandmother, and my mother. *Under the Ladder to Heaven* was, I thought, my entrance into this dialogue of Jewish women's voices.

The dialogue grew in the 1980s. I had discovered contemporary writers such as Irena Klepfisz and devoured her first book of poetry, *periods of stress*. Klepfisz, a Holocaust survivor born in Poland during World War II, wrote directly out of the Yiddish tradition I was just learning. I was even lucky enough to hear Klepfisz read her bilingual Yiddish/English poems at UCLA Hillel. Klepfisz was a co-editor along with Melanie Kaye/Kantrowitz of *The Tribe of Dina: A Jewish Women's Anthology*. In the *The Tribe of Dina* I discovered Enid Dame's poems in the voice of Lot's wife who was transformed into a pillar of salt. I did a reading in Los Angeles at the National Council of Jewish Women with Marcia Falk, poet and translator of Yiddishe women poets, and a number of other Jewish women poets.

In the mid-1980s I started to write more poems about both Biblical women and twentieth century forgotten Yiddish-speaking women. I wrote of Biblical women who had been maligned or had bad reputations: Bath-sheba, accused of being a tart; the Witch of Endor; and Vashti, Queen of Persia, the archetypal bad wife. I also wrote a series of poems about European Jewish women who fought in the Resistance against the Nazis. These women needed to be remembered also. Browsing through a women's bookstore in San Francisco I discovered the novel *Deborah* by Esther Singer Kreitman, Isaac Bashevis' sister who was a forgotten writer. After reading *Deborah* I was moved to write a poem about Kreitman's tragic life.

In the 1990s we Jewish women writers had our own magazine and anthology. My prose poem "My Aunt Sara's Shoes" appeared in *Jewish Women's Literary Annual,* published by the National Council of Jewish Women in New York. Reading this magazine, I discovered many voices close to my own writing about my Yiddishe grandmother; poems about other Yiddish women; and poems in the voices of Biblical women such as Leah, Rahab, and others. Lilith seemed to be appearing everywhere and even had infiltrated popular culture through the Lilith rock 'n roll festival. The second part of my poem "Lilith" was published in the anthology *Which Lilith? Feminist Writers Re-Create The World's First Women*, edited by Enid Dame, Lilly Rivlin and Henny Wenkart.

When I received the anthology, I was surprised to see my poem included in the section "Lilith and the Family." Enid Dame in her introduction to this section surprised me even more when she said about my poem, "But some midrashic poets can and do imagine Lilith as both wild woman and successful parent." For the first time I reflected that I, too, was writing poems as midrash. In my midrash Lilith is not the demon who steals babies from cradles but rather the good mother who provides a home for outcast and runaway children. Outcasts and runaways have to go somewhere! It seemed perfect that the leading female outcast would provide runaway children with a home. Now that I had a poetic "home" I could write in the voices of Jewish women over the millennia. Thus I wrote the rest of the poems in *Shulamith* in the 1990s.

A Short Bibliography

Anderson, Elliott, editor. "Contemporary Israeli Literature." *TriQuarterly*. Spring 1977. Number 39.

Dame, Enid, Lilly Rivlin and Henny Wenkart, editors. *Which Lilith? Feminist Writers Re-Create The World's First Women*. Northvale, New Jersey: Jacob Aronson, 1998.

Jewish Women's Literary Annual. Prepared by The Jewish Women's Resource Center, a Project of the National Council of Jewish Women New York Section. Volume III. 1998.

Kaye/Kantrowitz, Melanie and Irene Klepfisz, editors. "The Tribe of Dina: A Jewish Women's Anthology." *Sinister Wisdom*. 1986. 29/30.

Klepfisz, Irena. *periods of stress*. Brooklyn, N.Y.: Out and Out Books, 1975.

Koltun, Liz, editor. "The Jewish Women: An Anthology." *Response*. Summer 1973. Number 18.

SHULAMITH

EVE FORGIVES

Adam, I first distrusted you for telling me different
stories of how I was born. Once you said the Lord created

us both out of the dust of the earth. Once you said
the Lord put you to sleep, took out your rib

to make me. The snake hissed at me that you had
a first wife before me called Lilith and said

I would never know of my birth until I ate from the tree
of good and evil, the tree the Lord told us not to touch.

For days I pondered the snake's words and
came back again and again to the forbidden tree,

picked two scarlet fruits, caressed them in my hands,
smelled their perfume, held them up to my eyes,

until I took my first bite. Then I knew as if the dark
was lit by lightning. You saw me eating,

grabbed the scarlet fruit and devoured one.
We heard the Lord walking in the garden and ran

away to hide from his anger in the bushes.
When the Lord called out, "Where art thou?"

How could you stumble out of the bushes stammering
I had lured you into eating from the tree? Liar!

When the Lord told me I would labor to bear children and
you would rule over me—see what pain your lies

caused me! I suffered when the Lord drove us out
of the garden, chased by cherubim with flaming swords.

I ached on that long march to a new home, sweated in
those animal skins we had to wear, bled from

the thistles when we cleared our first piece of land,
screamed hours giving birth to our first son Cain.

Now you tenderly hold the howling baby in your arms.
I'll forgive you and put down my anger.

LILITH HAD A DAUGHTER
for Thomas McGrath

Mother of all outcasts,
    the first outcast who ran away
        from the Garden of Eden heard
        her daughter Aviva say, "Mother, let me go,
        let me leave your garden."
        Lilith held back
her tears, gave the girl food, waved goodbye,

saw Aviva shrink
    smaller, a dot on the
    horizon trekking across the desert.

Aviva walked on a dusty Judean road
    when an angel saw her,
        stopped lifting weights,
        hid in the bushes, jumped on her back.
        Aviva threw him to the ground. Up
        that angel jumped.
        Back Aviva pushed.
    "What's your name?" the angel asked.
        Aviva clamped her mouth shut.

Aviva grabbed him,
    swung him round and round with all her force,
        threw rocks at him,
        he flew up to disappear,
                and with a shout she began to climb
                  the ladder to heaven.

                    She climbed up to the clouds,
                    to the roof the sky where
                a gang of angels waited
                for her at heaven's gate, holding
            ropes they threw at her. She
                ducked and dived. The angels
            circled her, pulled their ropes tighter
            and tighter, caught her, trussed her
        dragggged
        her
    down to
earth.

Her face forced down on the ground.
The archangel loooooomed over her,
a dark shadow whose voice bOOmed,
"You will be forced into slavery,
a bartered calf, condemned for generations to
silence,
only speaking with her tears."
She cried thousands of tears.

HAGAR IN THE DESERT

How I missed my home Egypt, hated my slave's life
spinning, weaving, listening to my mistress Sara sob

she was a childless withered old fruit of sixty.
She ordered me to sleep with her husband. Yes,

I obeyed her, let Abraham come into my tent late,
after midnight he came, pulled me onto the sheepskins.

I perfumed myself with jasmine waiting for him.
Night after night I put flowers in my hair for Abraham.

Then I was with child, looked at Sara as my equal.
Sara no longer stood haughty ordering me around.

Her fist struck me and she beat beat beat me;
a shrieking demon of rage striking at me.

I ran into the desert, tears down my face, falling,
to the well where I cried in exile now twice.

All alone, nowhere I can call home, no family,
no friends. Is there no place for me in the world?

SARA'S LAUGHTER

I was a sorrowful well overflowing with tears
lamenting for years how I was barren as a rock.

A fool I was giving Abraham my handmaid Hagar;
the pain a knife tore at me each time I saw him

go into her tent. Hagar with her bulge of a
belly scorned me. Each look cut me. A tornado

of rage came over me so I hit her and hit her,
drove her out into the desert, then sat down and

cried at my life. Yes, those three beggars in black rags
at our tent had less than I, so I kneaded my best meal

and baked cakes on the hearth. At the tent door
saw three angels in white silk devouring my cakes.

One angel said I would have a son. I laughed
and laughed again when my flat belly started

to grow with child, felt Abraham's hand on it
and the love in his eyes, a love I had forgotten.

LEAH'S CONSOLATION

Sister Rachel how I envied you your sweetheart
that first day you two walked back from the well

tied by an invisible thread. My envy grew
for seven years Jacob worked to marry you.

I loved his muscles his hands his face
but he never once looked at me.

No suitors came to woo me, the ugly one.
Yes, I plotted with father to steal your veil,

your groom, your wedding, sat happily by his
side at the wedding feast—my few hours with him

when his eyes drenched only me with love.
I kept my veil on in bed, only let him pull the dress

down my hips. These moments were mine,
his hands swirling round and round my body.

Only in the morning when he pulled up the veil
his eyes were shocked to see me and I cried.

For seven years I had him in bed every night.
Days his eyes followed you around with longing.

The children I bore—Rueben, Simeon, Levi, Judah,
Issachar, Zebulun, and Dinah—are my consolation.

RACHEL

Sister, I loved Jacob from the moment his brawny
arms pushed the boulder away from the well

letting my sheep drink; his arms circled me like a
bracelet and we kissed. The seven years

I waited for our wedding flew past on a wing.
My wedding night I was a bird you and father tied

to the bed and gagged. I hated you when you put on
my golden gown and covered your face with my veil.

All night I cursed you, hatred settled in my bones.
Finally I married Jacob, but hatred for you still coursed

through my bloodstream as I saw you, an overripe
apple tree, bear four sons while I was barren.

I screamed curses when you spat out two more sons;
at last I held my first child Joseph my love.

Now, pregnant I hear the omens are bad for this birth.
I watch your gray head, your watery eyes,

your tears from how Jacob scorns you for years.
Before I die, I want to drop this boulder of hatred

I've carried for years for my sister and let us be
friends for a few moments, oh, my sister.

DINAH SPEAKS TO HER BROTHERS

Once I was a carefree girl. Once long ago before
Shechem the Hivite grabbed me. I screamed

and beat against him even when he raped me.
Then he locked me in an upstairs room,

brought me sweet pastries, lamb meat and
kind words he tried to feed me. I spat at him.

He visited me day after day trying to smother
me with his kind words, told me his father and

my father had agreed on our marriage. "Never,"
I yelled. He babbled on and on how he and all the

men would get circumcised before the marriage.
Through the window I saw the knife tearing

at the foreskin. Hour after hour it went on.
For three days all the Hivite men groaned.

I heard shouts and screams from below. You, brothers,
Levi and Simeon, broke into the room, grabbed me,

lugged me through the mob of fighting.
Hebrew knives stuck like pins into Hivite men,

"Levi, Simeon, stop it," I pleaded. But you ignored me.
By the burning houses the women and children cried

as your men rounded them up. We walked among
the captured women, sheep, children, and donkeys.

My brothers laughed at their spoils. Only my father
Jacob held me crying in his arms. Only he screamed

at Simeon and Levi at the horror they had done.
Sweet brothers, you have doomed me.

The Hivite women ache to put a knife through me,
their eyes glitter with hatred at me. I won't wait for them,

will do it to myself, with this knife I hold above
my wrist. Once I was a carefree girl. Once long ago.

THE HARLOT BY THE ROADSIDE

Judah, how dare you scream at me I'm a harlot!
Point in horror at my three months' pregnant belly.

Threaten to burn me. After my husband died,
you promised to give me your third son as husband.

I waited in my widow's robes for you to act.
The Hebrew women in your tents scorned me,

the barren one, the Canaanite widow. I was afraid
you'd throw me out to starve alone in the desert.

So I covered my face with a thick veil like a harlot,
sat by the roadside with my breasts hanging out.

Remember, you gave me this signet, these bracelets,
and your staff before I let you lead me into the bushes.

Whose babies are in my belly? Yours! Now you
turn white remembering the night with me in the fields.

You admit I was more righteous than you, say I will be
one of your wives. Yes, I am, and yes, I will be your wife.

SHIFRA TALKS TO HER FRIEND PUAH

Where do my words come from? It's a mystery.
When the Egyptian soldiers bound us and dumped us

in the throne room I was mute, just heard Pharaoh's
voice thunder an order to us to kill Hebrew boy babies.

At the next birth I held the male baby in my hand.
When he cried, you looked at him so terrified.

The words jumped out of my mouth: "We'll hide
him and his mother in the cave near Goshen."

The soldiers came again, tied us with chains.
In the palace they made our faces lick the floor.

Pharaoh said in icicle tones, "Why have you let
the male children live?" His words froze my bones.

For the first time I raised my head, stared at
an old man, wizened and ugly in a purple shroud.

My words swelled up: "The women hide and give
birth before we come." Pharaoh waved us away.

Puah, I never knew where my words come from;
only I must obey them. Now let's watch the Hebrews

put on the roof of the two stone houses they build for us,
houses sweet as dates, sturdy as the pyramids.

MIRIAM'S SONG

I swept the house clean through nine plagues,
swept when Moses turned the river into blood,

swatted at frogs all day in the Egyptians' kitchen,
chased frogs in the bedrooms, whacked at them

on the beds, jumped after frogs in the kitchen. Next
I cleaned off lice from the heads of the Egyptians.

When my brother sent flies, the Egyptians had me
stand over their meals and beds swatting at flies.

After the Lord killed their cows, we laughed
even as we smelled that horrible stench.

Then I spent hours wrapping up the boils
all over the Egyptians' skin rejoicing.

The Egyptians made us women go into the fields,
round up their cattle, drive them into barns,

lock the doors against the pounding hail.
The day the locusts devoured the plants

I swept my house and swept three more days that
the Egyptians sat in darkness, for only we had light.

Before the tenth plague I swept once more,
then roasted lamb and cut up bitter herbs we ate

remembering four hundred years of slavery
that terrible night the Angel of Death screeched

and screamed as he flew over our houses
on his bloody way to kill the Egyptians' sons.

We were leaving so I baked my bread unleavened,
packed clay crockery, black pots onto a rickety cart.

I wanted to smash the pyramids.
We'd built them well. They'd last. A pity.

At the Red Sea, after we climbed onto the land and
saw Pharaoh lead his chariots into a gap

riding between two huge cliffs of water when
mountains of water crashed down on them,

I called the women who came with cymbals and drums,
"Come dance now for we are flying into freedom."

MIRIAM'S WELL

Thirty years we marched through
the dunes of the Sinai whenever

we were thirsty they'd circle me and scream,
"Miriam, find your well." I'd smell the air,

point my long staff, and, no water that day,
hear them braying like donkeys, giving me

no rest until, lo, there was my well
gushing with water, watched them rush

to drink. I'm an old woman, tired of my
people loud as angry crows stubborn

as asses I love them but I want to rest now how
I ache for our own land where I can sit

by my well surrounded by olive and date trees
feel the cool water gurgling down my throat.

RAHAB AT JOSHUA'S TENT

Joshua, I hated Jericho, despised all the hypocrite men
who flocked to me at night and avoided me in the day

and loathed the women who cursed me, spat at me,
called me a dog of a prostitute, kicked me on the street.

I lied to the men of Jericho, said the Hebrew spies
had left, and smiled like a cat as they ran all over town

searching for the two spies hiding under my roof.
I laughed as the townspeople cowered the seven days

the Hebrews circled Jericho blowing seven rams' horns.
On the seventh day I dressed in my finest linen robe

and gold necklace as the Hebrews sounded rams' horns.
The walls of the city fell flat. The people ran to hide.

I waited joyfully by the scarlet cord at my window, the sign
the spies had given me so their soldiers recognized me,

followed the Hebrews through the city in flames,
yelling, "Burn, Jericho, burn, Rahab is leaving!"

At your tent, Joshua, the first time I look at you I know
at long last I want to get married when you take my hand

tenderly. I am no longer Rahab of Jericho. Here, I will
join your people and worship your God. Here, I will live.

JAEL EXPLAINS

How did the body get here?
Heber, it's been here for hours.

After sunset last night I heard the horse hooves
and cries from the battle at Tanach,

milked all the cows and churned the butter,
prayed for you, my husband, to live

and for victory over the Canaanites,
lit the wood for a small fire by the tent.

That evening as the battle cries went on
I watched the stars shift to our side of the sky,

saw a man running to my tent.
Who was the man in the muddy blue tunic

of the enemy general standing at my door?
"Sisera?" I asked. He nodded, begged, "Water."

I brought him a clay jug of milk
he drank thirstily, then collapsed asleep

in the tent where I covered him with a blanket,
stood with nail and hammer over him,

watched him sleep like a sweet boy until
I hammered the nail into his temples.

He body fell to my feet dead. I sat and
waited for you to return as the sun rose.

DELILAH

Samson never stopped hounding me,
trailed me around the village for weeks
yelling he loved me. He was the first stalker,

this huge raging foaming bull of a man.
Once angry at his Philistine wife he set afire
three hundred fox tails in the middle of

Philistine corn so they burnt her house.
He ignited a war of Philistines against
Judeans, leaving blackness and blood.

His own people bound him with cords,
delivered him up to his enemies. Before the
blundering fool killed me I had to

shove him out of my life. No one bribed me
with silver. I did it alone, asked Samson,
"Where does your strength lie?"

He said, "Bind me with seven green tree
withes. I will be like clay you can beat."
He burst the tree withes like blades of grass.

I asked him again, then bound him with ropes
he broke like thread. I asked him a third time,
wove a web through seven locks of his hair.

He woke up, still the enraged bull
who charged out of my house. I told him
"How can one love me and lie to me?"

Samson poured out his heart, fell asleep
on my knees. I cut off his hair as he slept,
watched his strength pour out of him like sand

out of a pitcher when the Philistines bound him
and dragged the mad bull away. The stalker who
had hounded my days was at last conquered!

RUTH CONFESSES TO BOAZ

I had rather cut my throat than allow Naomi,
frail old woman, to walk alone on the

hard dusty road back to Bethlehem. Moab
was no longer my home. So we became homeless.

I carried our bundles, our feet ached and
we were hungry the long walk through the hills.

In the Judean fields I followed the reapers with scythes,
picked up bits of barley all day my arms in pain

and my throat parched for water. The Hebrews
broke my heart when they eyed me hostilely.

I hungrily watched them eat wheat bread when you,
Boaz, strode up to me, your huge shadow fell on me.

My heart mended when you sat me beside the reapers,
gave me bread and a clay jug of water, told me to glean

only in your fields as I was your kinswoman under
the protection of your wings and the Lord's.

Naomi clapped her hands when I brought her
the basket of barley and clapped again when I told

her of you, Boaz. Days I picked only in your fields,
my eyes fastened on your every move, my heart

a summer field overgrown with love for you,
the baskets full with barley and wheat for Naomi.

That night I joined the circle of your threshers
covered with barley, singing and passing wine jugs,

the first time in years I sang and drank red wine.
When you lay down by a heap of corn to sleep,

I felt I was a magnet drawn to you. Softly I
uncovered your feet and lay down as in a new home.

Midnight you awoke and asked, "Who are you?"
"I am Ruth." When you put your blanket over me,

I wished I could sleep forever beside you. At dawn
I had to kiss you once before I left your side.

Morning your eyes glowed at me like flaming embers
as you poured out for me six measures of barley.

Naomi and I waited all day in her tiny tent.
When the boy came yelling that at the city's gate

you had said you would marry me—I wept. Now after
our marriage your huge arms carry me over the threshold.

My heart is a well overflowing with joy.
I know I have finally found my true home with you.

THE WITCH OF ENDOR

Saul, your disguise doesn't fool me.
I know who you are, King of Israel.
How could I ever forget when you
screamed in the palace against the witches,

women who spoke out against your harem,
led mobs of men who skewered my sisters.
Only I escaped with my two daughters,
fled to this cave in Endor, this wilderness.

Now, you come to me when
your prophet Samuel has died cursing you,
half your followers have fled,
the Philistines are massed in battle before you.

You want me to call up the spirit of Samuel?
Promise you won't kill me for this.
Saul, long ago I stopped fearing you.
Wait, I'll call up the spirit.

Saul, stop screaming at my silence.
Oh, you threaten to kill me if I won't tell you.
Your threats are stupid. The spirit said,
"Tomorrow you and your sons will be killed."

You fall to the floor. Here, I'll help you up.
Come sit by the table. Eat this bread and meat.
You ride away desolate. Saul, the spirit said
your kingdom will fall like a jug that's smashed

but my daughters and I will live in
these barren caves in the wilderness with
our blackened pots, our babies, our prophecies
nurturing and sustaining our children.

BATH-SHEBA

All my sad nights I lay crying
over my life: I was a girl sold
in marriage to an ugly old man I hated.
How I wanted to kill myself when
your harp music drifted from the palace.
I let the notes flow over my body and
dam my tears. I heard your harp again
as my hands tested the bath water.

I let the notes guide my hands into
making slow waves with the water,
stood up. Your music rose with me.
My back to the window I could have
turned, closed the curtain. Instead
I let the music lift up my arms.
Unhooking my robe I felt the notes
caress my neck, heard your harp stop
for a second when I dropped my robe,

stood naked, sank into the soft water.
Your music spiraled swiftly
down my breasts, then slid softly
over my belly. The notes danced up
my thighs. When I stepped out of the bath
to reach for the towel your music poured
over me in a fountain of joy.

TAMAR

I was a good girl, obeyed you, Father King David
who sent me to nurse my sick brother.

Amnon watched me with lovesick eyes from
his couch in the kitchen as I kneaded flour and baked.

He told his servants to leave, asked me to bring
the meat pies to his bedroom. How could I say no?

Father, I followed your commands when I sat
on his bed, held out a meat pie to him.

When he ordered me to lie with him, I begged him
not to force me, pleaded him to go to you, Father,

to ask me in marriage but he grabbed me, pushed me
down on the bed. Afterwards, his eyes shone with hatred.

He had his servant bolt the door against me.
I poured ashes on my head, tore my clothes,

ran through the streets crying your name, Father,
wanting you to hold your daughter in your arms.

Father, why did you never punish Amnon?
Why did you bolt your door against me?

I was an outcast in my brother Absalom's house
two years with people shunning me in the streets

when Absalom and his men trapped Amnon
in Ba'alhazor where they killed the slobbering drunk.

I rejoiced and then shed tears when Absalom fled
to Geshur. Father, you cried every day for Absalom

for three years but you never once spoke to me.
Father, why have you abandoned me?

EVIL QUEEN VASHTI OF PERSIA

I never liked being queen, even if my husband
ruled from India to Judea, glad to miss
the king and his princes in the marble hall gorging
on cakes and pheasants strewn onto the pavement
of red, blue and white. I suffered through feasts
for the princes' wives, fat women dripping
heavy gold necklaces, chirping away like canaries.

The king showed off his jewels, his elephants, and
his tigers for the seven days of feasting. Then he sent
seven chamberlains to my feasts blabbing the king
wanted to show me off naked, with only a crown.
When I said "No," the women tittered and I heard
the king's screams three buildings away: "Now wives
all over Persia would show contempt to their husbands!"

When the kings' soldiers threw me into his dungeon,
I was relieved to be free of that prison of a harem,
grinned when the guard said I was no longer queen,
smiled again when I heard that the king had picked
a new queen, Esther. When the king hung his grand vizier
Haman the guards fled so I walked out of my cell
and escaped to this cave where I sit writing my memoir!

SHULAMITH

I am Shulamith,
the singer of songs,
of all the songs,
I am all the outcasts
for five thousand years:
the Hebrew women who
wept by the waters of Babylon,
the Romans threw me
out of Judea so I walked
bundle on my head,
baby in my arms
all over the Mediterranean,
I was kicked out of Spain,
walked up the boardwalk
of the stifling ship
fleeing to North Africa,
the Germans forced us
to walk East to Russia,
the Czar hated us,
one third he wanted to starve,
one third he wanted to convert,
one third he wanted to kill,
I ran to America,
a woman in exile.

I am the warrior
Deborah, the judge,
the trumpet who called
up the tribes to the battle
at Tanach, the boulder
that set thousands of
stones in motion.
I am Rose, union organizer,
the spark that set the women
in the sweatshops on fire,
on strike in New York.
I am the warrior muse,
Masha, ghetto fighter
from the Warsaw Rebellion,
packed like a sardine
on the train to Treblinka,
I ignited the men
in the death camp
with my stories
how I fought in Warsaw,
I was the match, the fuse,
the time bomb of revolt,
we torched Treblinka,
the camp buildings burnt,
I am running running
from the flaming camp
running to freedom
in the forest.

I am the lover,
my two eyes are
dark mahogany,
my long thick hair is
black woven silk,
my red lips are
full ripe plums,
my two breasts are
soft ripe pears,
my belly is
the softest pillow,
my two legs are
the sturdiest oaks.
I searched for
my lover in the streets
and avenues of the city.
When I found him
I took him back
to my house.
I covered his body
with my long dark hair—
I am the beloved,
the singer of songs,
of all the songs,
I am Shulamith.

THE MAID OF LUDOMIR

Oh, I could pray as if I were
a seed pod so filled up with holiness
I was about to burst open,

I could pray so strongly I could make
the angels laugh and the townspeople
gossip I must be possessed by demons.

When my mother died, God healed me
with a new soul. I put a white prayer shawl
around my shoulders and prayed so intently

my people in Ludomir chose me as their rebbe.
I preached every Sabbath, invisible to the men,
through a doorway, just a voice

that soared like the hawks in the sky,
a voice that the rabbis conspired to silence.
When I heard the rabbi of Chernobyl had

made a marriage for me and when they led
me to the groom, my voice withered away.
Only they couldn't stop me from waving

good-bye to my husband for the Holy Land
where I could pray for the time when
the voices of my daughters would ring out.

The Maid of Ludomir, Hannah Rachel Werbermacher, was the only female
Hasidic rebbe (spiritual leader) in Europe. Her story is told in Ellen Frankel's
Five Books of Miriam.

THE YIDDISHE DAUGHTER
For Esther Singer Kreitman

Her mother ailed on the couch,
her father preached,
her two brothers studied,
    she was the family maid, with her
        fainting spells, her hysteria,
      nearly mad, she said,
"Yes, you can choose my husband.
Yes, destroy the stories I wrote."
    Little tears of paper fell to the ground.

She put the golden necklace, a wedding gift,
    a lynch rope around her neck,
    the girl was a corpse under the wedding canopy
      silently saying
        "I am not your bride,"
    the marriage a graveyard,
for years she danced with the spirits of the dead.

The dybbuk stirred within her. She fled
    her husband in London for Warsaw.
Her mother only said, "You're so ugly,"
her famous writer-brother sent her back to London
    where the dybbuk helped her to write!
        and publish!
        THREE BOOKS!
    the British critics dismissed her, killed off her books.

Her writer brother lived to win the Nobel Prize.
She died forgotten,
turned into a dybbuk still flying over the land.

Esther Singer Kreitman was Isaac Bashevis Singer's sister and a novelist.
Dybbuk—a spirit that possesses a person. Also, "The Dybbuk" was a famous
    play of the Yiddish theater about a girl forced into an arranged marriage
    who is possessed by a spirit, a dybbuk. After the girl is possessed, she
    goes to the graveyard where she dances with the spirit of the dead.

DARK GIRL

Ashen haired
dark Jewish girl
mother of the starving ghetto
the burning ghetto
our lady of the bunkers
with her grenade
black hair huge dark eyes
too dark to have passed
outside the ghetto
leading her children through the sewers
to the dark forest

the dark ghetto girl
the last round-up
in the Warsaw ghetto resistance
beret on her head
herded to the death trains
squeezed in a car with eighty others
she pried loose a plank
jumped off the train
ran into the blackness of the woods

how dark
so dark she blends into the night
blends into the forest with the partisans
look for her
with her gun and her grenade
in the darkness of the forest
the starless black sky
you'll never find her
she still lives.

THEY FLY ACROSS THE GALAXY

Let me remember
  the Jewish women ghetto fighters in
  Warsaw, Biolytic, Kovno—all the ghettos,
teenage girls, mothers of the ghetto,
mothers of hope,
  send a letter to Zuviva, they said,
Zuviva, the mother of the Warsaw ghetto resistance,
  the hope for Polish Jewry,
      your every day was an act of courage.

Let me remember
      you were
  mothers bringing news,
      couriers who crossed outside the ghetto,
      the smugglers bringing guns in,
mothers caring for your children,
      you pulled them out of the line waiting
        for deportation,
mothers leading your children through the sewers
      out of the ghetto,
mothers planning revolts in bunkers to protect
      your children,
      you started to shoot at the moment of revolt,
      fled from the burning ghetto into the forests
        to join the partisans,
mothers who never abandoned their children.

Let me remember
                    the women I love the most
        the Jewish women partisans,
        in Russia, Poland, Italy, Holland,
                    parachuted into occupied Europe,
                    lit a fuse to blow up German trains,
            stopped to stand in the forest beside your male comrades
            from underneath a canopy of huge, thick branches,
        you smile at us, having your photo taken.

Let me cherish the women of iron, women of steel,
        the resisters at
                    Ravensbruck concentration camp
            miracle workers: Charlotte Eisenblatter and Olga Benario
                    conjured up an
                    all-women's resistance group,

        the resisters at
                    Auschwitz
            you talked your friends out of killing themselves,
            hid the sick from being selected for gassing,
            stole potatoes for them,
            smuggled babies out of the camps.
            took photos of the gas chambers, sent them out to
                        tell the world,
                    Rosa led the women at Auschwitz
            in smuggling ammunition out of the factories
                        to blow up the gas chambers,

the resisters at
>   Treblinka
>   Masha arrived with the Warsaw ghetto fighters
>   she was the lightning for revolt,
>   the spark, the fuse, the ignition,
>   the match, the warrior-muse,

look, the women put torches to death camps,
look, the camps are in flames,

>   smoke pours out to cover Europe,

ssssh, they run across the field to the forest,
>   bullets whizzzzzzzzzzzzzz
>   behind them,

they reach the trees
>   keep on running to the stars as
>   they fly across the galaxy.

FAIRY TALES

Once upon a time there were gas chambers and
crematoria; no one lived happily ever after.
"A Modern Fairy Tale," from Lawrence L. Langer's
The Holocaust and the Literary Imagination

I'm different from Estelle.
I was born after the war.
My mama told me fairy tales,
Sleeping Beauty, Snow White, Hansel and Gretel.
Estelle was born during the war.
A month later the Nazis
arrested her
father
in the big round-ups.
Her mother took her
underground.
She said she had no
fairy tales.
After the war
the people came back from
the death camps.
Her mother took her to them
to look for her father.
She was three years old.
The people were very
skinny.
Her mother kept on asking
if
they'd seen her husband,
No one had.
He never came back.
She had no fairy tales.
She doesn't believe in
happily-after-after.

I'M CHUGGING INTO FRANCE

How children sang
on the train chugging into France!
I sang like that
once in shule songs just burst out of me
in Yiddish, Hebrew and English.

Not in public school.
All the children at the Christmas assembly singing
only Christmas carols.
My voice began to
shr
   i
nk.
Once I made it into choir to diligently learn
"Oh come all ye faithful" in Latin.
My stout voice narrowed
into a thin tremor.

In the children's train passing through Nazi Germany
the Jewish children were
silent at the French border watching
in silence the Nazi soldiers take one child off each car
to inspect them the children
silently hoping the Nazis would
LET THEM
                    GO!

Shule—after-school or weekend school to learn Jewish culture.

The children burst into a storm of songs
    as soon as
        the train crossed into France,
        a riot a rampage of melodies!
        Listen!
            the whole train is singing
            the songs pushed the train
            faster into France faster!
I want to sing
        just like they sang
            crossing into France
            sing as I once
            sang in shule
            sing an old song
            my Hasidic ancestors
            used to sing,
            sing a ngonen,
            a wordless song,

                Bim bam Bim bam Bim bin Bim bam
                bin Bam bin Bam bin Bam
                    bin bin bin bin bin BAM!

THE GRAND TRADITION OF WESTERN CULTURE

. . . the Jewess has a well-defined function in even the most serious novels. Frequently violated or beaten, she sometimes succeeds in escaping dishonor by means of death, but this is a form of justice; and those who keep their virtue are docile servants or humiliated women in love with indifferent Christians who marry Aryan women.
Sartre, *Anti-Semite and Jew*

My girlhood was surrounded by flickering screens,
        rows and rows of books about
                adored blonde Gentile girls and evil dark girls.
        The hero always
                again and again he walks out on the dark girl
                for the blonde.
        I was a little dark Jewish ghost
no one would ever fall in love with,
        a ghost hovering in the
aisles of movies and libraries.

In *The Jazz Singer,* that great movie hit,
        the Jewish boy paints himself with black face,
        sings black folks' songs to white folks,
        becomes rich and famous,
        holds his hand out to his blonde girl he loves,
generations of movie moguls became
        rich from these movies,
        again and again they turn to their blonde bride.

These movies follow the Grand Tradition of Western Culture,
        Jewish girls herded onto a cart, a boat
                onto a train chugging chugging
                        out of the country to exile, to prison, a camp,
                        for centuries
                whole countries dumped the dark girls for the blonde.
        Their dark girl ghosts haunt us,
                whenever the movies are played,
                the books are read
        their ghosts
                will be in the aisles and rooms
                                        screaming.

CANCER'S IN THE HOME

My grandfather screamed from the stomach cancer.
  Cancer's in the home.
  Death's knocking on the door
 of our white trash shacks of West Los Angeles,
with the washing machine outside the kitchen door.
   My uncle took me at three years old to
      thick brown earth and stalks of green beans.
      The man in the overalls gave me a green bean.
      I wanted to go live with him.

The FBI knocked on the door of
   my aunt's New York apartment.
   The witch hunts came home.
   She's called witch.
She calls herself Communist, the first organizer of
the cafeteria workers' union. Small fish in the party.
   Her boss fired her.
      Her union wanted to expel her.
      The FBI trailed her to Los Angeles,
         my home, to spy
   on our very little shacks with my very
      sick grandfather.

My aunt and grandmother argue
   how much morphine to give my grandfather—
   he's still crying.
   Every time they left the gate unlatched
 I'd run away as fast as my fat
three year old legs could take me,
  to the man in the bean field
     where I wanted to live. They always
     find me, take me back. There's no escape
     when cancer's in the house.

GREEN ALGAE BISCUITS

My childhood best friend started to walk away from me
after her daddy got a raise and rode up in a new blue Chevrolet,
      My daddy drove a beatenup used black Dodge.
She's walking home laden with bags from shopping trips.
At junior high school she sat on the benches with her friends
      four peacocks in pink yellow blue cashmere sweaters
      and ignored me.

      Was it my clothes?
      No matter how hard I tried
      to save my allowance
      I could never afford to buy cashmere sweaters,
      buried myself in books,
      fell in love with my science teacher,
      shut out the world with my science projects,
      counted the years with sunspots,
      grew algae, baked them into biscuits
      —algae to feed the world—
      tried to eat those ugly green biscuits,
      got straight A's in my classes,
      graduation my science teacher on stage calls
      the name of the best science student—it's my name.
      I walked across the stage in a daze.

The first day of high school, I'm corralled by the benches
by four smart girls in blouses and straight skirts who were
the best math students and the editors of the newspaper.
"You eat lunch with us," they said.
      It's three years since I've had friends
      and I wanted to cry.
      Only years later realized I wanted to be
      with girls who baked green algae biscuits!

LET'S FLY TO THE MOON

Barbara, it's time to show off our wounds
proudly as our battle scars.

It's time to remember my sixteen-year old courageous
    heart set on a four-year liberal arts college,
    admitted with a tiny scholarship.
        Daddy said, "No! We don't have the money."
            We screamed verbal bullets at each other
            until I ran crying back to my room,
    got back into the ring for more fights
        for years for my dreams.

It's time to remember you at sixteen from the housing projects,
    your tough Jewish girl's heart set on a rich girl's college,
    You got the loan forms for your daddy to sign.
        He said, "No."
        You screamed for three days until
        he took the clock radio, said, "Stop screaming
        or I'll throw the radio at your head."
    You kept screaming; he raised the radio, put it down,
    signed the loan. You got back into the ring for more fights
        for years for your dreams.

We're veterans now, let's sweep
our old dreams together like broken shards,
mold them into a rocket and a launching pad,
an arrow aimed at our bull's eye.
As teenagers we wanted to fly to the moon.
Come, friend, we're stronger now
we won't let anybody stop us from
flying to the moon.

HER HEALING HANDS

The unsaid words were tumors
        festering under my skin
    too afraid to speak of
                hemorrhaging
    from an illegal abortion.

The unsaid words were nightmares
        repeated over and over and over and
                acids that corroded my life, afraid
    of getting attacked.

           Only
at the women's clinic, a safe oasis
        no one would attack me there, the nurse
            held my hand, the first time
   anyone
            ever held my hand,
                with her healing hands she
        wiped away my nightmares,
        cut out my tumors,
            the tumors
              vanished,
            the nightmares
              disappeared.

I AM THE MISSISSIPPI

Once I was an abortion clinic getting bombed regularly.
Each bomb they explode at a clinic detonated on my skin.
Too long I've been bombed-out rubble.
                              No more.

I will become the Mississippi River.
        My water will smother all the dynamite at all the clinics,
            will be a swell of water,
                a rainstorm,
                    a thundering rage,
                        a rampage of a river,
                        a great gush,
                            tons of wet wrath,
                                a churning flood.
        I am the Mississippi,
            an angry river,
                a flooding river,
                    a high-tide river,
                        a mean torrent of a river,
            an engorged river flooding over banks,
                smashing dikes,
                    shattering levees
                        ripping apart bridges,
                            watch out you people with bombs
                            I'm flowing your way.

I KNOW HER

Sister in desperation.
We were afraid the administration would ax our jobs.
She xeroxed grievances on the office machine—
our jobs restored like a forest of newly planted trees.

Sister in raising hell.
We wrote up a petition, stuffed it in all the teachers' boxes.
Silence for a month when Mr. Big wrote a letter,
apologized for not responding to us sooner.

Sister in holidays.
We celebrated Sukkoth, sat in a green booth made of
green leaves and branches, feasting on halvah, hummus, wine
—protected from all our enemies.

A sister you can rely on.
Often I opened the door to her room, let her students in.
Once I was late, the door to my room was open.
She can be counted on.

DID THE WORDS?

A Palestinian family lost
the brothers, sisters, uncles in one week of war in Lebanon
all that was left—
    two little girls with feet scorched by phosphorus,
    their mother,
    their two old male relatives,
all lying on the Beirut hospital floor,
all were speechless,
did the words leave,
    one by one
    as they lost each relative?

LORD, I CAN'T ESCAPE

Lord, what is this being Jewish
when I'm haunted at the supermarket
by the Palestinian in an Israeli jail?
I walk up the fruit aisles, see
the guard beat him and beat him.
Which oranges, navels or valencias?
Choosing six valencias I see him in
the prison yard, shaking in a blanket.
I weigh one of the cabbages, too heavy,
search through the pile for the smallest,
again his face in tears appears.
Lord, I can't escape, his cries corrode
my waking hours and disturb my sleep.

SOY MARRANA IN NEW MEXICO

I want to see the Hebrew inscriptions on the gravestones in
old Hispanic villages of New Mexico,
want to sing the Jewish songs in Spanish
that Sephardic Jews exiled in 1492 from Spain
have been singing for five hundred years,
want to learn what movements Jews gave to flamenco,
want to learn how to dance a Jewish flamenco,
want to learn how the Marranas secretly boarded ships in Spain to Mexico,
wandered their way north from Mexico into New Mexico,
oh tell me one thousand stories of the trip to El Norte,
want to whisper Hebrew prayers over a candle on Friday night
behind curtains so my neighbors can't see,
want to confess how each time
each time I downplayed my Jewishness
I, too, was a Marrana,
want to wallow like a fat pig
in the thick mud
of my Jewishness,
soy Marrana,
soy Marrana,
soy Marrana.

Marranos (masculine) or Marranas (feminine): Jews in Spain in the fifteenth
century who converted to Christianity often practiced Judaism in secret while
in public they were Catholics. In Spain they were called Marranos or pigs.
Marranas weren't allowed to immigrate to the Spanish colonies, but some
went to Mexico and then on to settle in New Mexico.

I'VE BEEN HERE BEFORE

Why do I see swastikas blossom all over
      Los Angeles this year?
      A swastika at the city college parking lot,
          on the freeway underpass,
two swastikas on my car door,
         swastika buttons in the shop window.
                        I've heard the news,
     the synagogue in Temple City was bombed,
       at the cemetery where my grandparents lie
     tombstones had been scrawled on.
                    I've been here before
        in some dream, some previous life,
    unemployment up, economy depressed,
blame the Jews.

MY MAGIC SHAWL

I. Eagles with Talons

My grandmother ached at her sewing machine
in the factory making clothes she could never afford,
paying for her younger sisters to go to school
she could never attend, and could watch with pride
her younger sisters graduate high school.
She hungered for this life she could never have.

In her life the rich ladies swooped like eagles down on
my grandmother, attacked her old cotton dresses,
said all my mom's skirts and blouses were wrong,
Their long talons shredded my mom's self.
My mother and grandmother accepted their cruelty and
their castoffs—navy blue suits and light blue rayon blouses.

II. Buttons

My grandmother taught me to always meekly take in
other people's castoffs and their insults, how to
mend by hand, sew on buttons, collect scraps of cloth.

I used to thread her needle when I was a child,
After her death, I kept all her buttons: pearl buttons,
gold buttons with mirrors on them, brown leather buttons.

From her I grew to love buttons and scraps of materials.
Later at garage sales I'd buy torn quilts I'd take home
to mend knowing my grandmother would approve.

III. At the Quilt Show

I was dazzled by quilts of flowers, stars, and log cabins;
stunned by a jacket of red pieces and a blue-white vest.
I knew I had come to my home with stalls of women
looking through stacks of fabric pieces they would take
home to piece together into more quilts.

I was drawn back like a magnet to the stall with
a long blue Indonesian shawl. What woman lovingly
designed the dancing blue-gray figures on the shawl?
When she tied on the black strings for a fringe did she
make it as her last piece before she went to work in a factory?

Like my grandmother does she give all her pay to her family?
All my life I have never bought clothes I loved, always said
I can't afford it. Today I bought this shawl, and knew
I would never again accept insults after I wore this shawl.
Wrapped in this shawl I felt like a queen in my glory.

1996

This is the year women started walking again.
In Los Angeles we are walking outside the big whale
of a shopping mall carrying picket signs to get garment workers
a union in our city which had Thai slaves sewing clothes.

We are the daughters of union organizer Fannie Sellins,
gunned down in a Pittsburgh mill yard,
whose hat was stolen from her dead body
by a deputy who laughed at her corpse,
whose death set off the Great Steel Strike of 1919.

We are the nieces of my aunt Sara Plotkin who walked
all over the coal fields from Pittsburgh to Wheeling in 1932,
put potato sacks on the windows to evade spies,
organized a huge crowd to demand food,
and who lived to tell her tale.

They whispered us their secrets, handed them down,
to daughters and nieces. We have their courage as our inheritance.
Just as our mothers and aunts walked across the coal fields
we have begun to walk across this land.

A WOMAN OF VALOR

Who can find a virtuous woman?
For her price is above the rubies
Proverbs 31:10

She's stitching a dream of justice
weaving it for five thousand years.
She gets up early to tend sheep
for wool and flax for linen,
her hands work with the spindle
and the distaff to make yarn,
spinning out her prophecies in
golden threads she weaves tapestries
of herstory to hang on the walls,
rugs that have blue and gold stars
of her people for the floors,
thick woolen blankets for the beds
to give warmth to her family in all
history's storms, sews white skirts
blouses and shirts so her husband
and children can be resplendent on
the Sabbath, sells her linen and wool
in the market for her daily bread.
She sews orange cotton for featherbeds,
stuffs them with goose down, sturdy
enough for thousands of years of
exile, pogroms, expulsions.

Her featherbeds she gave her
daughter leaving for America.
She poured into new textile mills
and sewing factories still spinning
dreams of justice fourteen hours
at her loom at her sewing machine,
sang for bread and roses on a picket line,
filled the paddy wagons and jails,
jumped out of a sweatshop on fire
arm in arm with her best friend
gave speeches on a wagon in the ghettos
for suffrage for her laboring sisters.
Her name was Clara in 1909
firebrand at the shirtwaist strike,
Rosie mourning in her speech the
Triangle Fire deaths in 1911,
Sara leading garment workers out
the doors onto the picket line in 1925,
the Common Threads women handing out
leaflets to stop sweatshops outside the
big beige whale of a shopping mall in 1996.
She sat down against sweatshops
in the streets of Seattle in 1999,
weaving a web of justice to entangle
all the whole world's sweatshops
sewing a blanket to cover the globe.
Give her the fruit of her hands
and sing her praises
she is a woman of valor.

Clara Lemlich—young Yiddish speaking garment worker whose fiery speech
    initiated the 1909 shirtwaist strike in New York City.
Rosie Schneiderman—garment union organizer who spoke out against the
    Triangle Fire deaths in 1911.
Sara Plotkin—my aunt who was a garment union organizer in New York City
    in the late 1920s.
Common Threads—anti-sweatshop women's group in Los Angeles in 1995–1996
    that picketed the Beverly Center shopping mall, among other actions.

LIKE HAGAR IN THE DESERT

In my childhood I was in two exiles
I had my Jewish exile from Israel,
and I was a Los Angeleno in exile from the Jews.
Rich alrightniks threw the Reds, my grandparents,
out of the LA Jewish community;
at the height of the Red Scare they were scared.

We huddled together for warmth
at the Yablon Center on Beverly Boulevard
where I went to Sholem Sunday school
learned how to sing Negro Spirituals—
"Go Down Moses Let My People Go"
I always thought was a Jewish song.
The earnest woman teacher read us
lists of stereotypes to teach us not
to be prejudiced with never a mention
of God or Zionism, the two black holes.
The Real Jews believed in God and Zionism
in public. I believed in God in
private, yet never knew how
to connect to them, the Real Jews.

I wasn't a Real Jew just an outsider.
Once I asked my mother to take me to
synagogue where they chanted Hebrew,
a foreign language I couldn't understand.
It took years of digging like an obsessed mole
to find my history of exile, years of failed
attempts visiting Hillels and synagogues
always the stranger in a strange land.

Until Nahid came banging on my door,
asking me to teach her daughter English;
again and again I turned her down
when I relented a little and spent
Shabbat at her house with streams of
Persian dishes coming out of the kitchen—
fish, cilantro, rice, chicken stew, tea—
reminding me of my grandmother's Friday night
dinners with the same deluge of food.

Nahid, the Persian stranger to America,
was the outsider in Los Angeles
full of all the Yiddish Jews—I was
the American Yiddish Jew insider.
I learned at her dinner table the blessing
over wine, how to say the blessing as I
pour water three times over my hands
out of a golden cup, say a blessing over
challah, egg bread, then dip it in salt.
I had come home to bread, wine, and prayers.

NOW I GET THE CHANCE

As a teenager I wanted a Jewish fairy godmother to rescue me
        from high school snobbery
                over fashion I never could afford,
                cars I could never own,
     years I dreamed of a fairy godmother
     to whisk me away.
     No one ever came to rescue me.
     I had to teach myself magic.

The girl's mother whispers to me
              she can't afford to give the girl
                    what her rich friends have,
     I tell her mother I'll tutor her daughter,
              this girl with great dark eyes
              in baggy overalls
    tell her daughter
        about vintage clothing shops
        show her the magic of
        creating her own vocabulary of clothes,
        show her the good, green world
        on her first hike up Runyon Canyon,
        explain Shakespeare's sonnets
        until she says, "He's wonderful,"
    show her how to sing her own songs
I can't wait.

EVE AND LILITH, TOGETHER

Eve and Lilith eyed each other suspiciously
after Eve came to the gate of Lilith's garden.
Lilith showed her the terraces of tangerine trees,
lilacs, orange groves, the cactus blooming
with orange, yellow and blue flowers,
the hundreds of children digging, watering, planting,
asked Eve, "Why have you come?"

Eve said, "For my children you stole. Adam says."

"Lies," Lilith screamed.
"Adam's a liar. He's been lying about me
for millennia. To scare you off.
Ask him. He won't deny it.
These children are the outcasts, runaways, throwaways."
Eve mulls this over.

"He lied so you'll always be docile."
Eve said, "Lies. I took the fruit. You talk about
lies but what lies you say about me. Yet I wondered
where the children in exile went. After Adam and
I threw them out I missed them so."
"Here. I gave them a home."

Eve starts to talk, then stops and laughs.
Lilith laughs with her.
They collapse on the ground with laughter,
laugh for days.
And Lilith flew Eve around the world.